LITTLE RED MONKEY

BY **Jonathan London**

ILLUSTRATED BY **Frank Remkiewicz**

DUTTON CHILDREN'S BOOKS ◆ NEW YORK

FOR AARON & SEAN & DAVID & LEAH & MAX—

the kids who like to dance to the "monkey rap"—J.L.

FOR RICHARD & PAM BROWN—

great friends & mentors of monkey painters—F.R.

Text copyright © 1997 by Jonathan London
Illustrations copyright © 1997 by Frank Remkiewicz
All rights reserved.
CIP Data is available.
Published in the United States 1997 by Dutton Children's Books,
a division of Penguin Books USA Inc.
375 Hudson Street, New York, New York 10014
Designed by Amy Berniker
Printed in Hong Kong   First Edition
ISBN 0-525-45642-2
10 9 8 7 6 5 4 3 2 1

THIS IS THE STORY OF LITTLE RED MONKEY,

WHO WAS BORN IN THE JUNGLE,

CAPTURED WHEN HE WAS VERY YOUNG,

AND LATER PERFORMED IN THE CIRCUS.

Little Red Monkey
was feelin' kinda funky.

He liked to dance
in his underpants.

He liked to dance
on a zebra's back

with his cape really flyin'
all shiny and black

or dance with a lion
singin', "Yakety-yak-yak,

don't give me no flack!"
No jivin', no lyin'——

that monkey liked the circus
but said, "Don't jerk us

around!" (A monkey in a cage
was like a dog in a pound.)

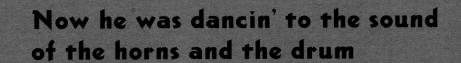

Now he was dancin' to the sound
of the horns and the drum

singin': A-rooty-toot-toot
and a bing-bang-bum—

blow your silver flute
and bang your silver drum.

And the tigers started roarin',
and our monkey started soarin'

on the flying trapeze
with the greatest of ease...

till he flew out the tent
as if heaven-sent.

When he landed on the ground,
he traveled all around

with a hurdy-gurdy man,
thinkin', I'll leave if I can.

**Then he hopped on a freighter,
seekin' somethin' greater.**

**In Yokohama
he did a dance in a drama.**

Then he went on to Moscow
and did a dance from Krakow:

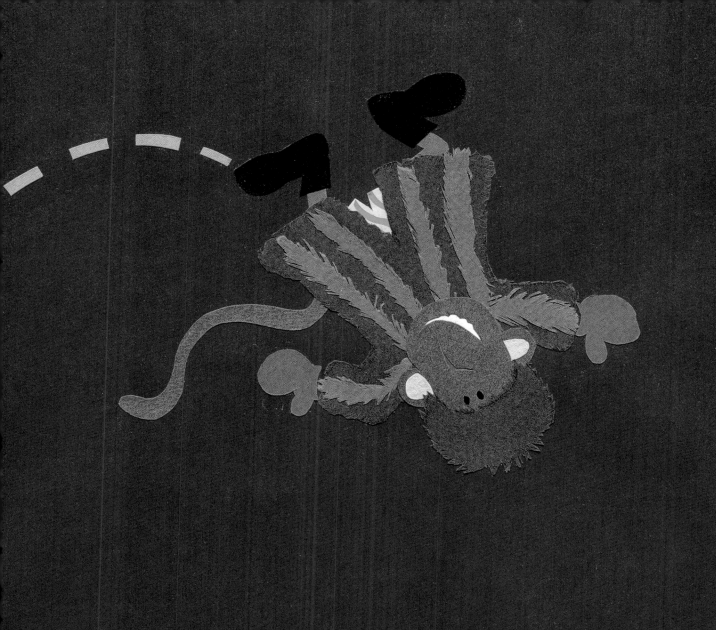

he danced the mazurka
till he went berserka.

Now he'd found some fame,
and Paris was callin'.

When he hopped off the train,
the rain was fallin'.

He starred in a show,
but the show fell flat,

so he passed the hat
with a really cool cat

who liked to jam.
But a rich madam

said, "You belong in a zoo!"

The keeper gave chase
—it was a wild race—

and the next he knew. . .

he was in Timbuktu!

In the desert with the camels
and other kinds of mammals,

he hopped a caravan
and said to the man

that his heart was torn:
should he live in a zoo,

where the livin' was easy
and the food was free,

or return to the jungle
where he was born?

What would YOU do?

Then before he knew it . . .
he was halfway through it!

He was back where the drum
made his heart really hum.

He knew sooner than later
there was nothin' greater

than to be dancin' as free
as a monkey in a tree!

Yeah, Little Red Monkey
was feelin' kinda funky.

He liked to dance . . .

in his underpants!